The Adventures of Pop Pop the Amazing Grandad and Pierre the Wiggly worm

Contents

Written and Published by Don Rose

ISBN 0-9549841-0-2

The Partnership

Once upon a time there was a Grandad who had a wiggly worm for a friend. Grandad was sitting in his chair in the garden one day, enjoying the sunshine when he heard a noise! No it wasn't a squeak or a whistle, a shout or a scream, but more of a wiggling sound coming from a hole in the nearby apple tree at the bottom of his garden.

Grandad looked around the garden and saw a wiggly worm sitting on a leaf wearing a beret on his head. Grandad nearly fell off his rocking chair when the worm spoke to him.

"My name is monsieur Pierre wiggly worm," he said, in a very deep French voice. "What is your name?"

"My name is Pop Pop, the amazing Grandad and this is my garden," replied Pop Pop.

Pierre explained how he had flown over the sea on a bird's leg, all the way from Paris in France. Pop asked Pierre what he did in France, so Pierre explained how he worked for the police helping children when they were in trouble.

Pop Pop said "Why don't we form a partnership, as I work for the British Police as well?"

The first thing Pop Pop did was to build Pierre a tree house in the apple tree for Pierre to live in, with a large yellow slide for him to quickly reach the ground. In the tree house he built Pierre a bed, a kitchen, a living room and a cupboard with a hook to hang his beret on.

Pierre moved in and was very happy in his new home. Pop Pop also gave him a mobile phone so they could keep in touch when they were helping the police.

The very next day, Pop Pop got a very urgent call from Amber, his Granddaughter, to say her pet rabbits, Sugar and Spice, had escaped from their cage and run away. Amber said that they were nowhere to be found, and she was very worried about them so could Pop Pop and Pierre look for them.

Pop Pop called Pierre on his mobile and told him about Sugar and Spice. So they set off in Pop Pop's old van, taking with them Pop Pop's box of tricks in case of emergency.

When they arrived at Amber's house, Pop Pop said he would look up on the hill, while Pierre looked in the valley.

The rabbits were nowhere to be seen.

Then Pop Pop had an idea. He got the kite out of his box of tricks, and let it sail high up in the sky on the very long rope. He then tied it to the gate post and asked Pierre worm to climb up the string and look for Sugar and Spice with his big binoculars.

Pierre climbed up the string and looked all around with his big binoculars, he then shouted down to Pop Pop that the rabbits were nowhere to be seen.

"Come down, and we will look somewhere else for them," Pop Pop called up.

They packed up the kite and went somewhere else.

First they tried the football ground. No rabbits!

"Then they tried the golf course. Still no rabbits!

So they carefully crossed the road, looking both ways before crossing. They then looked in a big field where Pop Pop thought he saw some movement coming from one corner.

Pierre climbed onto Pop Pop's shoulders and looked through his very big binoculars. "It's them!" He cried.

Pop Pop called Amber on his mobile and she came to the field with her mother to get the rabbits back. She put them into their travelling box and gave them a good telling off before taking them home. That just left Pop Pop and Pierre to pack up and return home very happy and hungry, they had dinner and then went to bed.

The Flood

One cold and windy day in December when Pop Pop and Pierre had nothing to do in the garden, it was so cold and wet that Pierre the worm had to live with Pop Pop in the house as his house was frozen up.

Pop Pop made Pierre a little bed from a small box with a blanket and pillow. They sat in front of the big log fire talking about past adventures when the phone rang. Pop Pop got up to answer it, "Hello said a man on the other end, this is the headmaster at the local school and we need your help."

The Headmaster explained that the school bus was stuck in the rising water of the flood from the river. All of the Children and the driver were stuck on board and were very scared. Could he and Pierre please help them. Pop Pop said that they would be right there, so wrapping up warm with coats, hats and very large wellington boots, they set off in Pop Pop's van.

On arrival they noticed the water was already half way up the bus and the school children were calling for help. Many people were stood around but did not know what to do to save the stranded children and driver. Pop Pop got out his box of tricks and undid the lid, he peered in but could not think what to do, then Pierre came up with an idea.

He went up stream grabbing the rope Pop Pop had got out of his box of tricks. He waited for a stick to float by in the raging water and bravely jumped onto it. Pop Pop let out the rope bit by bit so he headed towards the bus.

"Pull me in the window." he said in his deep French voice.

So the children did so and he tied the rope to one of the seats inside the bus. By now the water had risen much higher and there was no time to waste. Pop Pop pulled out a harness from his box of tricks and asked Pierre to pull it to him.

One by one Pop Pop pulled the children back to safety, followed by the driver but then the bus was swept away, where was Pierre! Pop Pop shouted and as he did he heard Pierre, who had jumped into the drivers pocket.

This had taken quite a while and everyone was very muddy and exhausted. The crowd cheered Pop Pop and Pierre for their brave feat and thanked them very much.

They returned home wet and cold, but happy with what they had achieved.

Several days later the weather improved and the Postman called with a letter from the Queen to ask them to come to the Palace and receive a bravery award for helping the children and driver of the bus escape to safety.

When they returned the school threw a big party for Pop Pop and Pierre, with all the children and their parents. They both felt very proud that they had saved the day.

The partners now had new business cards printed by Pop Pop's son Nigel, with the heading 'By Royal Appointment. Detective and rescue Specialists.' Pop Pop also had a large Brass plate fixed up on to the gatepost and Pierre had a smaller one fixed to the tree outside his tree house.

The Holiday

Pop Pop and Pierre worm had such a busy time lately with rescuing and helping children at all of the local schools and giving lectures on their adventures and road safety, they decided it was time for a holiday.

The summer had not been very good this year, so they decided to go camping and have a rest. The first thing Pop Pop had to do was make Pierre a hammock, so if he got tired of travelling he could have a sleep in the van.

Pop Pop got tickets for the ferry and they packed the tent, sleeping bags, stove and other equipment into the van. Pierre packed his own bag with his water wings, which go around his wiggly body and bright red swimming costume, bucket and spade.

The plan was to go to France and visit Pierre's relatives on the farm in Nice; he was very excited and could not wait to get going.

They arrived at the sea port Calais and drove Pop Pop's old van with all of the camping gear along the road. People waved and cheered as they drove along because the French papers had the Bravery story on the front page. The headline was Viva Pierre the Wiggly worm and Viva Pop Pop.

Pierre kept a notebook of all the interesting things they saw as they drove through the villages and towns. They had a long drive as

Pierre's relatives lived in Nice, right at the bottom of France.

The first night they camped in a field, after Pierre asked a farmer if it was OK. The farmer had a long conversation with Pierre in French with much hand waving and gestures.

They found the field and put up the tent. Pierre wasn't much help as the wind kept blowing him up in the air when he was trying to hold the tent down. Pop Pop had to do the whole job on his own and after hitting his finger with the mallet, he finished. While Pop Pop did the tent Pierre cooked eggs and bacon for dinner, which they both enjoyed. Pop Pop put Pierre's hammock up in the top of the tent and they both went into a deep, deep sleep.

During the night it rained and rained and rained. In fact it was still raining in the morning, so Pop Pop and Pierre decided to have a shower in the rain. Just as they had both put soap all over, it stopped raining, so Pop Pop had to wash Pierre in a glass of water and himself in a stream.

The farmer laughed when they told him later.

After another days driving, they arrived in Nice in the evening to be greeted by Pierre's relatives kissing them on both cheeks. Pierre's relatives were winegrowers so they had some wine with their dinner. There was an empty field by the farmhouse so they camped there for the night.

They planned to go to the beach the next day, if the weather was fine, and Pop Pop was going to sunbathe to get a tan. Pierre was already brown so he didn't want to sunbathe, just swim and play on the beach.

So in the morning, Pierre was up bright and early with the cockerel crowing on the rooftops. He was dressed in his red bathing costume, water wings around his body and his beret proudly placed on his head and carrying his bucket and spade.

Pop Pop and Pierre spent several days at the beach making sandcastles and swimming in the sea.

At the end of the week the townsfolk laid on a big banquet and dance to celebrate the visit by the two Hero's. Pop Pop and Pierre danced with all the ladies and had a great evening.

The next day Pop Pop's van broke down so they phoned the French railway to see if they could take them and Pop Pop's van home to England.

After spending a great time with Pierre's relatives they waved goodbye, with more cheek kissing and returned home on the train.

When they arrived they found a large package on the doorstep from the School, thanking them for the bus rescue.

The Naughty Bird

It was spring and Pop Pop and Pierre had lots of work to do in the garden, cleaning up the winter leaves and sticks that had gathered around the flower beds and in the hedges. The Daffodils and crocuses were just coming out into bloom and the trees were covered with blossom. The birds were nesting in the trees and hedges and singing away all day.

The garden was a happy place but Pop Pop and Pierre worked very hard and were tired so they got out the deck chairs and Pierre made some lemonade with slices of lemon and ice in a large jug.

They sat under the Cherry tree at the back of Pop Pop's garden and watched the chickens scratching in the leaves. The chickens spotted Pierre, as they like worms, so Pierre kept his distance while Pop Pop put the chickens in the pen. They were just dozing off when Pop Pop heard the phone ringing. He got up from the deck chair with much moaning and groaning and went indoors to answer the phone.

It turned out to be the chief of police; he explained that there had been several burglaries around the area where Pop Pop and Pierre worm lived. The chief of police asked if Pop Pop and Pierre had time to investigate as the police had a lot on at the moment. Pop Pop said they would, so the Chief of Police gave Pop Pop and Pierre a list of people to visit.

Pop Pop agreed and the very next morning they set off. First they called on Mrs Brown at number 17. They knocked on the door of Mrs Brown's house and Pop Pop explained why they were there. Mrs Brown said the police had phoned to say that Pop Pop would call to investigate her loss. Mrs Brown invited them in and gave them tea and biscuits while she told them what had happened. She explained that she had not gone out of the house on that day and that she kept the ring on the dresser in her bedroom and did not know how it had gone missing. Pop Pop wrote all the details down in his notebook and they left thanking her for the tea and biscuits.

Next they called on Mrs Smith at number 21. She was a plump woman with very blond hair, an old fashioned dress and a very high pitched voice. She asked the duo if they would like a cup of coffee and some home made cake. She explained that she used to be an opera singer and had been given lots of Jewellery by admirers who had come to hear her singing.

After an hour of her telling Pop Pop and Pierre about her opera singing days, she told them that she had not been out of the house on the day of the burglary, the doors were locked and she had a pair of earrings mysteriously go missing.

This had also happened on the same day as Mrs Brown's burglary.

Two streets away they called on Mrs Green. She also offered them tea and cake, and because they were too polite to refuse they ate the cake while Mrs Green told a similar story as that of Mrs Brown and Mrs Smith. Pierre got hiccups and Mrs Green told him to hold his breath and it would go away. She had a large parrot in a cage that kept on squawking 'Pretty Polly' and also hiccup noises just like Pierre, which made the three of them laugh and cured Pierre's hiccups.

The last person they visited was a young mother with two children called Mrs Donaldson. She also offered them food. She asked them if they would like some Dumpling stew and a drink as it was lunch time. Explaining that they had already had several items to eat, they declined. She told them that she had a gold bracelet stolen that she had purchased as a present for one of her children. She had also not been out of the house that day.

They left Mrs Donaldson's house wondering what they could do next to find out who had taken all of the Jewellery.

The next morning very, very early, Pop Pop was making some tea. He looked out of the window just as the sun came over the hill tops, there was blossom on the trees and while Pop Pop looked at the garden he spotted a large black bird, flying to its nest, carrying something in its beak that glinted in the sunlight.

Pop Pop remembered from his school days, that there was a large blackbird called a jackdaw, which stole items that glinted in the sun, like bottle tops and especially jewellery. He called out to Pierre who was sleeping in his tree house, to get up and dressed as they had a job to do.

Soon Pierre appeared at Pop Pops door yawning. Pop Pop explained over breakfast what he had seen, and the fact that he had remembered about jackdaws and there liking to sparking objects that were light and could be carried from peoples houses.

Pop Pop had a good idea. Why didn't he keep a look out for the jackdaw and Pierre could climb up to the nest and get back the stolen items? There was only one thing wrong with Pop Pop's good idea; jackdaws also like to eat worms so Pop Pop said he would shout in plenty of time for Pierre to get out of the way.

Pierre went up the tree to the Jackdaws nest and it was like a treasure chest, full of beautiful necklaces and trinkets. Pierre grabbed them quickly throwing them to the ground and climbed back down the tree before the jackdaw came back.

Meanwhile Pop Pop collected the items up and put them in a bag ready to take to the police station to be claimed by their owners.

The police would also need to put an advert in the paper to warn people to keep their windows closed at nesting time.

It was three cheers for Pop Pop and Pierre and thanks from the police chief.

"Before you go," he said, "would you like some cake and some tea?"

Pop Pop and Pierre said "no thanks," to his kind offer and returned home.

A good day and another mystery solved.

The Fishing Trip

It was some weeks later when Mrs Donaldson's husband phoned Pop Pop and Pierre to ask if they would like to go fishing in Hastings, as he owned a large boat. Pop Pop asked how long the trip was for and Mr Donaldson said the trip was for one week. He said it was as a thank you for getting the Jewellery back.

So Pop Pop and Pierre went shopping. Pierre bought himself a stripped T-shirt and a sailors cap and Pop Pop got himself a captain's hat, lifejacket and a pair of deck shoes for grip. The Donaldson's said that they planned to leave on Saturday and as it was only Wednesday Pop pop and Pierre had plenty of time to shop and pack before they went. The Donaldson's also said that Pop Pop and Pierre could follow them down to Hastings in Pop Pop's old van.

The van had spent several weeks in the garage being repaired, after it broke down in France when they were visiting Pierre's relatives.

With several days to go, Pop Pop and Pierre went to the loft to get down Pop Pop's fishing gear and other bits and pieces. Pop Pop then made Pierre a fishing rod from a large straight stick and a cotton reel. They then cleaned the van, checked Pop Pop's box of tricks and got everything ready for the trip.

Saturday morning came and they were up early, Pierre locked up his tree house and they awaited a call from the Donaldson's.

The phone rang and Pop Pop announced they were on their way. The Donaldson's arrived outside and Pop Pop and Pierre followed them to Hastings. The Donaldson's had a large people carrier for all of their luggage and children to ride in. The journey to Hastings was very pleasant as it was summer and the sun was shinning and the countryside was a sea of green.

On the way they stopped to have a picnic in the woods, the children played football with Pop Pop and their mum and dad. Pierre was in goal, as he could not run, only wiggle. After they finished they packed all of their chairs, tables and rubbish into the van and people carrier and set off again for Hastings.

Arriving late in the afternoon at the harbour, the Donaldson's pointed out a large boat moored in the harbour. Pop Pop explained "That is a large boat and it looks most comfortable."

Pierre asked how they got out to the boat and Mr Donaldson explained how they used a dingy to go out and then Mr Donaldson would bring it to the Harbour side to load and board safely.

Pop Pop and the Donaldson's unpacked all of the gear and when the boat arrived they took it onboard. The boat was very nice with large decks and inside it looked just like a house with a lounge, dinning room, Kitchen and three bedrooms. Mr Donaldson told Pop Pop and Pierre that the Kitchen was called a galley.

The Donaldson's suggested that as they were going to spend a week together that perhaps they should all use their Christian names. Mr and

Mrs Donaldson said that their names were Joe and Pat and their children were Daisy and Derek. Pop Pop said his name was Don and of course they new Pierre. Joe said that they would all need to board quickly to catch the tide.

Pop Pop and Pierre's cabin was quite large, Pop Pop hung up Pierre's hammock between two book shelves and they stored their clothes and fishing tackle away in the cupboards and were ready to sail. Joe had said to them that as soon as they were ready, to come up to the bridge for drinks.

Pop Pop wondered if he needed to put on his life jacket but Pierre reminded him that they hadn't yet left the harbour, so it might be a bit early for that. After drinks, Pat had organised dinner and as they left the Harbour they all sat down and had their meal.

Pop Pop and Pierre went up on deck to see the stars in the night sky, they twinkled very bight.

When they returned to the Dinning room pat had sent the Children to bed, Pop Pop and Pierre decided to go as well, because it had been a long day. Joe informed them he intended to go to a cove down the coast that he knew and would anchor for the night, ready for a swim in the morning. Joe told pat he would have his dinner then.

In the morning Pop Pop and Pierre awoke to the smell of bacon and eggs cooking in the galley. Everyone was up and moving about the boat. Pop Pop had slept in his life jacket, which had kept him awake due to being quite lumpy.

While Pop Pop, Pierre and the Donaldson family had a lovely breakfast, a fisherman hailed the boat. "Ahoy," he said. "I have just pulled up my Crab and Lobster pots and have plenty, would you like some?"

They all said yes, although Pierre didn't like the look of the Crab and Lobsters sharp claws and he kept well away from them.

The rest of the day was spent fishing, swimming and having a picnic, consisting of Crab and Lobster salad, on the beach. It was a glorious sunny day and Pop Pop and Pierre thought how lucky they were to be able to share this with the Donaldson family.

Pierre was the first to catch a fish that day, although very big as far as Pierre the worm was concerned, it was too small to keep, so they threw it back. Pop Pop had to tie Pierre to the deck rail while he landed the fish as it would have pulled him in the water.

At the end of the day everyone had caught a fish and they had a large basket of them.

"Why don't we visit France tomorrow?" Joe said. This pleased Pierre and made him change his sailor's hat for his beret.

Everyone put on their life jackets and Joe set sail for Calais. It was quite a long journey and the sea was getting rougher. Joe asked Pop Pop to take a turn at the Helm and steer the boat while he rested. Pop Pop thought this was great and kept a steady course for France. When Joe returned to the Helm he asked Pop Pop and Pierre if they would take watch as it was now getting dark.

They took up place on deck and after a while Pierre said he could see a light flashing SOS signals. It became clear that someone was in trouble, so Joe diverted the boat and headed for the light. As they drew nearer Pierre said the boat was sinking and there was a shouting noise. Pop Pop could see a man and a woman and two children waving their hands in the air. Pop Pop ran down to the cabin and grabbed his box of tricks and came back with the harness and rope they used to save the children from the bus. They drew alongside and Pop Pop shot the rope and harness across to them on a fire rocket. They tied both ends to the handrail and while Joe kept the boats level, Pop Pop pulled them all to safety. Luckily the sea had calmed down as they were near to France, but just after the man was pulled onboard the other boat began to sink, so Pop Pop cut the rope and they all had to watch the boat sink. It was a sad sight but at least everyone was safe.

The man introduced himself and family and told them they were from the Isle of Wight.

"You're a long way from home," said Joe, We will turn around and take you home."

While they headed for the Isle of Wight, Joe radioed the Coast Guard to meet them in the Harbour. Taking them back meant cutting the trip to France short, but at least they had saved the family from disaster. When they arrived in Harbour there was a welcoming party and everyone cheered as they pulled into the dock and let the family off. What an adventurous trip they had had with the Donaldson family and as they returned to Hastings Harbour, the press was waiting for them to take lots of pictures for the papers.

School Sports Day

After travelling around the country in Pop Pop's old van lecturing and giving talks to children on safety, both at school and at home, Pierre and Pop Pop arrived back home to find a lot of post on the door step. In fact there was so much that Pop Pop had real trouble opening the front door, so they had to go into the house through the back door.

After picking up the letters and sorting them into order, Pop Pop plonked himself into his favourite rocking chair and started to open them. Pierre sat on the coffee table and waited for Pop Pop to start reading them out. They were mostly bills, but Pop Pop's eyes were immediately drawn to one with a large crest on it. This turned out to be an invitation to the local school's sports day and as they had saved the children from the bus, they would be honoured if Pop Pop and Pierre could come to be judges and also hand out the prizes.

Pop Pop called the headmaster and told him that they would both be proud to come and assist in the sports day event and what day was it so they could plan it into their diary. The headmaster told them it was at 09:00am on this Friday, as that was end of term for the children. Friday soon arrived and as usual they were both up early. Pop Pop had decided to wear his old school blazer, that just happened to still fit him, and Pierre wore his Beret and scarf.

On arrival at the school they were greeted by the headmaster who detailed how the day would go and then showed them to the sports ground where all of the sports gear was laid out on the ground ready. There were coloured flags all around the grounds and tables had been set out on the edges of the field for all of the silver shields, cups and badges to be put on.

Pop Pop picked a couple up and saw that they were all very old and had been used for a 100 years with students names on for each year they had been won. It had been the schools 100th anniversary the year before as Pop Pop remembered the celebrations and carnivals.

On one side of the sports ground they had erected a tent for refreshments and another for a rest area for the children, with a first aid person in case someone was injured. There were lots of chairs for the parents to sit on, one row after another. On the back of the school was a picture of Pierre in his beret and gown, this had been taken and put up because the school had made him their mascot after the bus rescue.

The children were all ready in their sports gear and trainers to take part in the sports day. A great cheer went up as Pierre went out onto the field to start the first race. This was going to be the three-legged race, where you tie one of your legs to someone else's and have to race as a team to win.

Pierre held the starting pistol up and the children chanted Pierre the worm, hip, hip hooray. With that Pierre squeezed the trigger and the race was off. The children ran down the marked out course, some falling along the way and getting up again and others rolling around on the ground unable to get up. Eventually the race finished, by which time Pierre was back at the presentation table and he had a black face where the staring pistol was fired.

The rest of the races took place one by one, mainly started by the sports teacher or Pop Pop. There were four teams red, green, yellow and blue and they all had coloured shirts on. The headmaster was really pleased as the sun shone and everyone was smiling. However, pretty soon a small cloud appeared in the sky, then another, then a large black cloud followed by some thunder and lighting.

Everyone ran for cover into the refreshment tent and had a drink while the torrential rain, thunder and lighting stopped. When the rain stopped some time later, they all went back outside and realised that someone had taken the largest trophy, a big silver cup, which was 100 years old.

"This was for the best team effort and could spoil the day," the headmaster told Pop Pop and Pierre. "Could you please look into it while we finish the day and hopefully you may solve it before the presentations take place."

Pop Pop and Pierre decided to head for the woods at the other end of the sports ground, while the headmaster searched around the school buildings. They found an old log and sat down to think and listen to see if they could hear anyone. After a while they heard a sneeze and a clink of metal on the ground behind some bushes. Pop Pop and Pierre carefully crept toward the bushes and pushed the leaves apart. They saw a man sitting on the ground with a large silver cup beside him. Pop Pop and Pierre decided to jump the man as he was quite thin and didn't look like he would put up much of a fight.

Pop Pop jumped onto him, while Pierre twisted his nose and ears. "I give up!" the man said.

So Pop Pop and Pierre took him and the cup back to the school. They arrived back at the presentation table just in time, the headmaster was so relieved that they had found the cup. The headmaster called the police who took the man away for questioning and the presentations started to take place.

First, there were the individual events and then the best team. That was won by the blue team. Pop Pop presented the trophy and everyone was happy.

After everyone had gone the headmaster once again thanked Pop Pop and Pierre for capturing the thief and returning the cup. They both went home exhausted from their busy day and had dinner, then sitting down to relax watched some television.

Pop Pop

Pierre

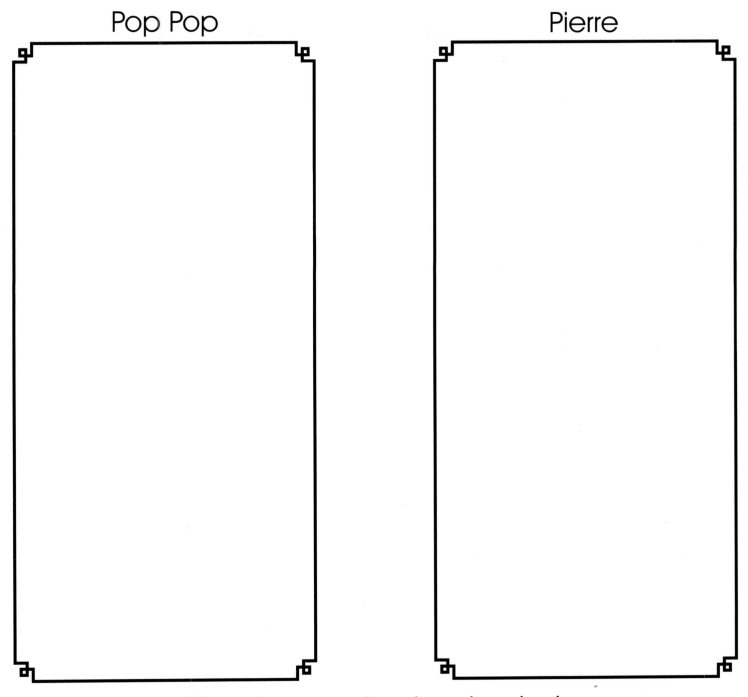

You draw and colour in what
you think Pop Pop and Pierre look like.

The Xmas Break

As it was the school holidays, Pop Pop and Pierre decided to travel in Pop Pop's old van to visit Pop Pop's old home in Somerset where he used to live.

It was called Chapel Cleve just down the road from the sea called Blue Anchor Bay near Minehead.

They travelled all-day and booked into a pub called the Blue Sailor Arms.

The Manager on reception asked Pop Pop if he required a double or a single room as he could not see Pierre on the floor. Pop Pop gave the manager his card, which had a royal crest on it, the manager instantly recognised them by this, as by now the pair had become quite big celebrities all over the country.

The manager said "you are now known as the modern day Sherlock Holmes and Watson". They both smiled and acknowledged the manager's observation. However Pierre said he didn't really want to be known as Dr Watson, so Pop Pop said how about Dr Pierre, he smiled and said that he liked it.

The bellboy showed the pair to their room and Pop Pop gave him a small tip for carrying their bags. They had a shower, got dressed in their best clothes and went to the restaurant for dinner. After dinner Pop Pop called the new owner of Chapel Cleve on the telephone and introduced himself as a past owner of the house.

The current owner Mr Bean, was so pleased to hear from one of the past owners that he invited Pop Pop and Pierre around to collect a set of key's. Both Mr Bean and his wife explained that they were going away for Christmas and as Mr Bean had found some pictures of Pop Pop when he owned the house, he knew who he was. Therefore would they like to look after the house for a week while they were away. Pop Pop and Pierre said they would be delighted.

The next day they checked out of the hotel and after thanking the manager, drove over to Chapel Cleeve, where Pop Pop used the very big heavy bunch of keys to open up the large oak doors at the front of the house.

They both went in and Pop Pop found their way to the two spare rooms Mrs Bean had laid out for them. After they had hung up their clothes, Pop Pop said he would show Pierre around and they went to a room that used to be called the Key Bar. Pop Pop explained to Pierre all about the building and It's long history, he explained that it used to be a Chapel used by the Monks of Old Cleeve and it had many cellars beneath it to accommodate the sleeping quarters for the Monks at night. He added that next to the building was a Mulberry tree that is several hundred years old, the Monks used to get silk worms from it to use their thread to weave tapestries for the walls, they also made clothes from the silk. Pierre said he liked old things, as he had Pop Pop with him all the time, they laughed and Pop Pop continued with the history of the building.

He explained about a legend that there is an underground passage leading to the new Monastery a mile away from this building, however no one has ever found it. He also said that the original chapel was built in 1455 AD and the attached building was put up in 1800 and finished in 1900, so it was actually three buildings made into one. He explained to Pierre that the grounds outside also belonged to the building and the field to the front had Pop Pop's two horses and a donkey in it when he was the owner. There used to be very large hedges to the front of the house and a maze made from the hedges, which was easy to get lost in. But the new owner had taken all of these out. There were also lots of roads and chalets for people to live in on the grounds. All of the roads led to the house and then to the entrance, which had two very large iron gates with the family crest on each.

They were very heavy and took two people to open. Pop Pop and Pierre then got up and decided to look around the rest of the building while Pop Pop told Pierre about the rest of the rooms inside. First they went into the back bar and Pop Pop showed Pierre a secret panel in the fireplace where many years ago people used to hide secret papers, to Pop Pop this was a fairly small space, but Pierre could easily fit in and it was like a small secret room to him.

Pierre came out with a small copper coin which he found on it's side wedged in the back of the secret panel, it was a George the third half penny dated 1774. "Wow", they both said, "I wonder who hid that there." They decided to look it up later in a coin book Pop Pop had at home.

Next they went into the ballroom where they used to hold weddings and large dances and down a hall past another bar into the restaurant, then into the kitchens and then into the cellars. It was spooky in the cellars and Pierre didn't like it, so they decided as it was getting dark, to go upstairs and get changed to go back to the pub to stay and have some dinner. Pierre felt happier there with the bright light and the big inviting log fire. They sat down next to the fire and ordered a snack to eat, while Pop pop told Pierre some more about the history. Lots of people in the bar kept looking at Pop Pop and Pierre, as their pictures had been in the newspapers recently when they had been presented a medal from the Queen.

The next day they planned to visit the cellar in daylight, even though Pierre was trying to wriggle out of it. After their breakfast which consisted of bacon and eggs and a glass of orange juice, they climbed into Pop Pop's old van and headed for Chapel Cleeve taking the large bunch of keys with them.

When they arrived there was a coach in the car park full of school children. They went to open up the front doors, when one of the children shouted "It's them! Pop Pop the amazing granddad and Pierre the Wrigley worm" and they all started to run over to the front door where Pop Pop and Pierre stood.

The school teachers that were looking after the children arrived shortly, as they walked over. "We came in the front gate on the off chance," one of the teachers said, "to look at the building as we are studying Chapel Cleeve and It's history at school."

After the excitement died down and Pop Pop had told them the history about the building and all about the monks, Pop Pop told them he used to live there and the present owner had gone away and left him with the keys to show Pierre around. Pop Pop said he didn't think the owner would mind if he gave the children a guided tour around the inside of the building. The children all cheered and shouted yes please Pop Pop. He phoned the owner to ask if it was OK, the owner said no problem as long as they behave themselves.

The teachers asked the children to all keep together as they walked around the house and to follow Pop Pop. One of the children who was quite small said, "Please sir! Can we have our lunch first". They agreed and Pop Pop showed them to the ballroom where they could all sit and have their lunches.

The children all sat on the highly polished floor, that people used to dance on and Pop Pop, Pierre and the teachers all sat on a couple of benches that were along one of the walls. Pop Pop told the children that while they sat and ate their lunches they could ask him some questions on the house. So they did, Pierre was so tired he fell asleep on the bench, snoring away. He awoke with a grunt and all the children, Pop Pop and the teachers laughed. Pierre smiled and let out a yawn.

When they had finished lunch they cleared away all their mess and put it in the bins outside the back door. The first place they visited was the fireplace where Pop Pop had found a map of the house many years before, and Pierre had found the old coin. Pierre went back in to show the children where he had found it, but he came out covered in dust and cobwebs as he had fallen over.

Next they visited the old restaurant which seated 107 guests when it was a hotel. The walls were all wood panelled and the ceiling had wonderful patterns on them. Pierre was lifted up on someone's shoulders so he could have a better look. They then decided to go upstairs via the spiral staircase, with ornate carvings on the banisters and a beautiful oval window with coloured leaded glass in the ceiling above.

The steps creaked with age as they stepped from one to another. The teacher counted the children through the oak door at the top of the stairs and they found themselves inside an upstairs landing. Again it was wood panelled with ornate ceilings and oak doors leading off in every direction. Pop Pop explained how these used to be servants quarters when the house was privately owned. But they had later been converted into very nice Hotel rooms.

They then decided to go and visit the old Cellars which meant they had to go back down stairs. On the way they looked at a bell hanging up from the days when the servants lived in the rooms. Who do you think had to ring it? Yes you guessed it, Pierre, with a wiggle on the rope. The children all cheered again and they continued down stairs into the Kitchens.

The teacher asked the children to go back to the coach and get their jumpers as it would be cold in the cellars so when they returned Pop Pop opened the door. Inside it was very dark, so he put the light on, there were some very steep stairs going down to gravel floor. The teacher asked the children to all keep close as it would be easy to become separated in one of the many passages that led off.

A couple of the boys decided to make ghostly whispering noises, which made everyone laugh.

They entered a room some way down the passage and Pop Pop told the children and teachers that this is where the Monks used to sleep. "It is directly under the old chapel," he said, "so no *monk*eying around."

They all came out of the room and started to go further up the passage, when there was a sudden noise. "What's that?" said one boy.

"I don't know," said Pop Pop.

Then it happened again. A cold wind ran down the passage and the cellar door slammed shut, switching off the light. Some of the boys screamed. "Don't worry," said Pop Pop, "it is only the dark." He reached into his pocket for a torch and they all returned safely to the Kitchens.

"Can we go back to the coach," they said.

The teacher said "Follow me, but before we go let's count the children. All present and correct," he said.

Pop Pop and Pierre decided to investigate the noise, so they stood at the door and listened, it came again and again, "I'm off," said Pierre, "the ggggghost is coming to get us," he stammered.

"Don't be silly, there is no such thing!" said Pop Pop, "you get inside my jacket pocket and we will go and investigate."

They moved around the cellar until they could hear the noise behind a large black door. Pop Pop slowly opened it and shone his torch inside the dark room, by this time Pierre was looking over the flap of Pop Pop's jacket pocket. "There it is," he said, "and it is coming closer, look at its eyes."

Pop Pop shone his torch again and he thought it was a ghost, but before he could do anything else it jumped at Pop Pop. Pierre wiggled back into his pocket and Pop Pop put out his arms, it landed on his arm and Pop Pop grabbed it, at this point they heard a meow. "It is a small black kitten!" exclaimed Pop Pop, "it must have been locked in before the owner left for his break. Poor thing is probably more scared than we are."

They took the kitten upstairs to show the children what the ghost really looked like. The children were all sitting in the bus ready to leave when Pop Pop arrived in the car park. The bus driver opened the door and Pop Pop explained what had happened. "So you see how your imagination easily runs away when you are scared" he said.

The children and teacher roared with laughter and the kitten let out a meow. With that they all said there goodbyes. The teacher thanked Pop Pop and Pierre for the tour and they left to take the children home to their mothers. Pop Pop and Pierre took the kitten back to the kitchen and found some cat food and milk in the fridge, so they gave it some of each. The cat purred with delight.

Pop Pop phoned the owner and told him all about their adventures and of course the cat, the owner said he was sorry, but Pop Pop didn't think he was as he was laughing. Pop Pop said he would put the keys through the big old letterbox, when he had locked the doors, as they were returning home that night and that they would return another day and take the owner and his wife out for dinner as a thank you.

So they returned to the hotel paid their bill and drove home.

The Scout Camp

When Pop Pop and Pierre arrived back from the Christmas break he found lots of cards and a letter from the school, and the boys he met at Chaple Cleeve, Inviting them to their yearly camp in the summer holidays in July.

The letter said that they were very short of help to look after the boys and would Pop Pop and Pierre help out.

Pop Pop used to be a scout many years ago and asked Pierre, if he had ever been a scout in France?

"No," he said, "tell me all about it."

Pop Pop explained that it was a movement started by Baden Powell in the 1st world war to teach boys the good things in life, discipline and to all work together for the good of man. They meet once a week and wear a uniform of a neckerchief and woggle, a beret and shirt with all their badges earned by passing tests. Tests for first aid, making fires and living with nature and helping each other.

Pop Pop phoned the scout leader and agreed to help out when the time came. The scout leader said he would send all details by post and the dates.

Pop Pop and Pierre spent that evening getting all the old photo's out and looking at them. Some of them were very old going back to Pop Pop's boyhood days. Pierre was sorting through them when he found one of Pop Pop in scout uniform. In those days the scouts wore a hat like the Canadian police mounties wear. Pop Pop said "keep that one to one side and we can show the boys what I looked like in days gone by."

So Pierre put it on the fire place shelf. Pierre said, one thing that he already had was a beret, so he only wanted a shirt and a woggle and perhaps they might give him a badge or two to sew on his shirt. Pop Pop said "You have to earn all the badges."

Pierre asked if they have a badge for wriggling and Pop Pop said "No."

As it was only January, Pop Pop and Pierre had lots of work to do in the garden. Seeds to sow, pruning to do, as lots of trees had to be cut to let the sunshine into the flower beds and of course the chickens had to be cleaned and new straw for their laying boxes as they had just started to lay eggs again after the winter. So they both kept very busy.

In the autumn Pop Pop and Pierre were very busy picking all the fruit in his garden. Pierre was a great help as he could wriggle up the branches to pick the apples, cherries, pears and gooseberries. Pop Pop made up a rope and basket threw the rope over the branches, put Pierre in the basket and pulled him up to pick the fruit, after several weeks they had gathered all the fruit and Pop Pops kitchen looked like a fruit market. The next job was to sort all the apples into trays to store in the loft. The cherries and gooseberries took the longest, they needed the stalks cutting off and putting in jars, Pierre didn't get many done as he was eating more than he put into the jars so Pop Pop had to do most of it himself. Pop Pop told Pierre about the time he went to camp when he was in the junior scouts called the cubs. When he was young he was afraid of the dark, at night when he was sleeping in the tent and wanted to go to do a wee it was so dark outside that he went to the doorway held back the flap of the tent and weed just outside the tent. Doing that for two weeks got him into the habit, when he got home to mum he slept in a room with the bed next to the window so in the night he woke up for a wee put his hand out and felt the curtains and thought it was the tent flap door, he stood up in a sleepy way and weed all over the window, his mum heard a running watery noise and came up to see what was going on. Naughty boy he didn't earn a badge to sew on his arm for that. I wonder what sort of badge it would have been? Maybe a picture of a potty. Both Pop Pop and Pierre were looking forward to the July camp. The next day they got up early to get on with the gardening. They both cleared a spot in the garden away from the apples trees to make a fire to burn up all the broken branches and leaves after the pruning. They were both glad of the work as it was very cold after Christmas. They soon warmed up after pulling and cutting branches to the fire. Pierre said as we have a fire why don't we put some potatoes in the red hot ashes to have them with some beans for lunch, so they did.

Pop Pop told Pierre to keep his tail away from the fire otherwise he would be eating his tail with the beans not the potatoes. After having a good old feed with the beans and potatoes they were full up and went in to have a rest in front of Pop Pops log fire and both fell asleep.

The next day and several days later they had finished all the garden and could now start planting seeds and flowers, so that in the spring and summer the garden would be a picture of colour. So the days went on and July soon came round, Pop Pop got his letter from the head master to arrive at the school at 8 '0' clock on Monday 20th July. To leave his old van in the school car park and travel with the teachers and boys in two coaches to Whitstable in Kent to camp in a big field at farmers Browns farm. Farmer Brown had lots of animals cows, sheep, chickens, pigs, ducks, horses, a border collie called "Roxi" and a donkey called Pickles he was brown and white and came from Abyssinia. They arrived just after lunch and soon had all the tents up and sleeping bags out. In the field was a shop, a building for washing, showers and a place to cook with some toilets at each end. Pierre said to Pop Pop " I hope you don't do what you did when you were young!" Pierre said he wouldn't sleep near the tent flap door. Early in the morning all the scouts, teachers and Pop Pop and Pierre went across the field to wash and then to give a hand with the cooking they would ring a bell when breakfast was ready.

After breakfast they put up a programme with the whole weeks activities on it. There was hiking, races, walks and paper chases. Games and talks around the fire and singing. Lots to do so no-one got bored and every day they did a head count so none of the boys went missing. Pop Pop and Pierre were kept busy helping out with all the activities. Pierre slept like a log and Pop Pop didn't do bad either. There was a river on the edge of the camping field with trees and the boys made swings from the boughs to swing over the river and drop into the water, great fun was had by all. In the evening after role call they all sat around the camp fire eating sweets from the tuck shop and singing, each boy including Pop Pop and Pierre had to do something to entertain. Pierre had bought some gob stoppers they were big round balls, as you sucked them they changed colour. Pierre kept taking it out of his mouth to see what colour it was. After lots of singing by the boys and teachers and scout leaders It was Pop Pops turn so he sang old Mcdonald had a farm with a moo moo here and a moo moo there, everybody joined In. Most of the week was spent like this and every one enjoyed everyday.

On the last evening at story time by the camp fire, Pierre thrilled everyone by telling them all about his work with the French police before he met Pop Pop and there was absolute silence when he told them how he used to go bungee jumping from the Eiffel tower at night. The next morning it was into the coach and back home for everyone. Pierre had earned a special badge for his story telling and he wore it very proudly on his arm.

The Well Rescue

At the end of the road where Pop Pop and Pierre lived, there was what used to be an old pub that dated back to 1650. The brewery had sold it off to a family with two children, one called Henry, he was ten, and one called Billy, he was four, and their mum and dad. Pop Pop had got to know them quite well as David the dad kept chickens the same as Pop Pop and quite often came round to Pop Pop's garden to talk about gardening and chickens. They also went round to David's garden, as his wife Penny was a very good cook and good at baking bread, so Pop Pop and Pierre would take round flour and yeast so that when Penny was baking, she would make Pop Pop and Pierre extra loaves of bread. Sometimes she would bake currant loaves as this was Pierre's favorite he would have it for breakfast and toasted with jam.

There was never any left for Pop Pop when it was freshly baked, so Pop Pop had to cut the loaf in half and hide his half so Pierre wouldn't gobble the lot down.

It was some time later that Pierre came up the garden path to say that something was very wrong at David and Penny's house, as there was a fire engine and a police car outside the old pub. So telling Pierre to follow, he ran up the road to David's house where he saw lots of firemen and police in the back garden. When Pop Pop arrived he saw David and Penny looking very shocked and pale standing

When they arrived in Wellington, Pierre said "Did it get its name from the Duke of Wellington or from the boot?"

Pop Pop said "It's one of the same."

They were greeted with the same gusto as in Auckland, but this time they had to attend a gala dinner and dance in their honour.

The dinner in their honour was a very grand affair with a firework display afterwards. Pop Pop and Pierre were yawning their heads off with tiredness after such a long day and were very glad to get back to the hotel and get into their beds. They didn't even say goodnight!

The next morning after a good night's sleep, they were up early and down to breakfast as they had to travel down to the ferry and on to south island to Christchurch.

Arriving at the ferry they were shown to their cabins and told that dinner was nearly ready in the restaurant and also that they would be sitting at the captains table as guests of honour. This they did and had a great time talking to the captain about his naval career and Pop Pop and Pierre's adventures. The captain said "What an interesting story you all have to tell on your adventures and rescues."

They had just gone to the lounge for coffee, when it happened. All the lights on the ship went out.

The captain was called up to the bridge urgently. A net had fouled the propellers and the ship had to stop it's engines. That meant they were drifting in the open sea, very dangerous in the dark, with no electricity, no radio to send a message for help. The captain was at a loss to know what to do.

Pop Pop said to Pierre, "Go down to the cabin and bring up my box of tricks."

So he did and when he arrived back Pop Pop opened the box and got out a walky talky radio. He said to Pierre, "Go and get your beret and your wind cheater jacket and your binoculars and come back here quickly."

When he arrived back Pop Pop said, "You are good at climbing Pierre, so up the mast to the top and take my torch with you. Also the walky talky leave the other one with me so that we can talk to each other."

So up the mast went Pierre to the crows nest where he could keep a look out for other ships and warn them with torch to keep away and also tell Pop Pop and the captain what he could see.

The crew and engine room people were working flat out to repair the engines and as they were drifting around the shipping lanes, the captain had all the crew around the ship as lookouts.

Pierre called down on the walky talky to Pop Pop that he could see a light coming and what should he do?

Pop Pop said "With the torch, signal three short flashes, three long flashes and three more short flashes." ('S.O.S'). With that the ship turned away from them.

Pretty soon a search light appeared not far off and Pierre called down to Pop Pop that there was a large tug boat heading their way. Pretty soon a voice was heard saying "Ahoy ferry boat, stand by to take a tow line on board." Then a small bump as the tug boat came up to the ferry boat and a cable was sent over with temporary lighting for the ferry boat and a tow line was fixed to tow the ferry on to the south island. In the meantime Pop Pop called up to Pierre to climb down from the crows nest. Pierre was frozen stiff and Pop Pop had some hot drinking chocolate waiting for him inside the cabin.

They reached the harbour side and it was still dark so Pop Pop and Pierre made a bee line for the hotel to a warm fire another hot drink and into a warm bed.

In the morning Pop Pop and Pierre slept in late as they were so tired. So when they appeared at lunch time, the news papers were out in the hotel and the headlines were "Dramatic Rescue At Sea" Pop Pop and Pierre appeared on the front page with a full story of the incident.

After resting for a couple of days, Pop Pop and Pierre went onto Christchurch where of course, the lecture was all about the ferry boat rescue.

The last lecture they had to give was at Queenstown, to V.I.P's, and a trip on the lake and a party on board given as thanks to the pair, with all the thanks from the New Zealand people.

The Australian Tour

The minister of New Zealand education, when It was all over in Queenstown, came over to Pierre and Pop Pop and thanked them for a successful tour and said that everyone had enjoyed the whole program and hoped one day they would return to New Zealand.

The next morning after the ship docked at the edge of the lake, was spent getting ready to travel to Sydney, Australia, to begin the next lecture tour which would start in the north shore of Sydney, at a place called the Spit.

A very nice townhouse had been booked on the Spit, which was an inner harbour marina called Battle Boulevard, and again Pop Pop and Pierre were supplied with the same arrangement, a car and card to pay for petrol and food expenses. They were told they would have a weeks rest after the hectic time in New Zealand.

The town house was very nice and overlooked the marina and bridge where there were repair docks and lots of boats and truly wonderful place to stay and relax.

They were told the next morning that they were to be at the marina at 10 '0' clock to be taken on board a very nice cruiser, to take them on a tour of the Sydney harbour and the opera house. So Pop Pop said not to bother with breakfast as there would be food laid on for them on board the cruiser. So Pierre just washed and cleaned his teeth and put on his beret as protection against the sun. Pop Pop wore his captain's cap that he had when they went on holiday with Mr. Donaldson, on his boat.

The cruiser was a fifty foot luxury boat with all mod cons and was supplied by a promotion company with lots of female models, food and wine all laid out on tables. On deck there must have been forty people on board also the crew of nine. They left the Spit and slowly cruised past Clontarf beach, where years ago there was a pier, before the bridge was built.

As they reached the outer harbour they could see Bondi beach from the fly bridge of the cruiser. Cruising up the harbour to the Opera house was a sight indeed. Over on the left was Kirrabilli beach where the governor's house was almost opposite the Opera house. I think Pierre had had quite a bit of wine to drink as he looked a bit red in the face, or maybe it was the sun.

Pop Pop also was quite merry and spent most of his time talking to the ladies and had quite a few pictures taken with all the girls around him, some sitting on his knee. What a day! They had something to remember for a long time to come.

The return journey was made by taxi over the harbour bridge to arrive at the Spit and home.

The tour when it started was to take them up to Brisbane to lecture there, then back to surfers paradise. They would then fly them by sea plane to Adelaide and onto Perth and then home to England. After the Sydney harbour tour, they were due to arrive in Brisbane for their first lecture the following week but were told they would visit Torronga zoo first where Pierre was to make a small film, for publicity as a fund raiser for the children fund.

Pierre had to be filmed sitting on several different animals' backs, he said it was a bit high up on the camel's back and would not sit on the giraffe's head and nothing would persuade him to go into the crocodile pen either.

But he loved going into the rabbit area, as he remembered Amber's rabbits Sugar and Spice.

Pop Pop also was in the film, he had to dress up as a gorilla but didn't like the way the real lady gorilla was looking at him, so he quickly took off the outfit.

They duly arrived in Brisbane to their first lecture and talk and then onto surfers paradise to look at all the tall tower blocks. One was completely round and one called the golden gate spent most of the day watching the children surfing and a barbecue on the beach after.

Pop Pop and Pierre were taken up to sea world where they watched the dolphin show and afterwards lots of children came up to Pop Pop and Pierre for autographs and photographs standing with Pop Pop and Pierre.

In the afternoon, Pop Pop had a game of golf at surfers paradise golf club while Pierre had a sleep in the hotel as he didn't like golf.

In the morning they were taken to the wharf, and by small boat, out to the sea plane. It was a bit choppy, therefor making it a bit of a job getting from the boat and into the plane. Pierre nearly fell in the sea, but Pop Pop just grabbed him in time. They strapped themselves in and the pilot, whose name was Stan, welcomed them. He then explained the safety drill, which he did in case of an emergency.

It was a lovely hot sunny day as they taxied out to take off and they were soon up and away. Stan said it was quite a long journey to Adelaide so to make themselves comfortable and there were drinks and coffee in the picnic basket between the seats, also bottles of water. Stan kept in touch by radio to their destination reporting on progress.

The drone of the sea plane soon sent Pop Pop off to sleep, with Pierre looking out of the window. Pop Pop woke with a start as the plane started to rock about a lot and Stan was busy on the radio calling "May day, May day," the emergency call. He called back to Pop Pop and Pierre, to put their seat belts back on, as he was losing height rapidly. Down below they could see a small island with a beach all round, it was quite a small island. Stan said he would have to make an emergency landing as there was something wrong with the engine.

By this time they were getting quite low. Stan said to put their heads between their legs and their arms over their heads and would do his best to land. He was losing a lot of speed and the engine had cut out. Then there was a loud bang and a bump as the plane ran up onto the sandy beach, Stan was thrown forward and was knocked out.

Pop Pop and Pierre were O.K. so Pop Pop opened the door and jumped out onto the sand with Pierre beside him. Throwing out his box of tricks as he jumped, he then looked around to see if the plane was in danger of fire.

There was no smoke and no flame, so it looked as though they were safe for now.

Pop Pop said to Pierre, "We had better get up again to look at Stan the pilot, now there is no danger of fire." So Pop Pop climbed back in to the cabin to look at Stan.

He was still knocked out and was just coming round as Pop Pop reached him. It looked to Pop Pop as though he had broken his leg,as he was moaning a lot. When he finally came round he said to Pop Pop "My leg, my leg."

Pop Pop said to keep still' and he would look at it.

The way it was twisted around he could see that it was broken. Pop Pop gave Stan a sip of water and said keep still. Shouting to Pierre he told him what he had found out.

They now had to find a way of getting Stan out of the plane and onto the sand and try to set his leg. Pop Pop told Pierre to look around the beach to see if he could find a plank or something to make a slide, to get Stan out of the door.

He opened his box of tricks and came across the harness he had used in the bus rescue and a rope. Pop Pop called to Pierre not to bother with planks as he had found a way to get Stan out of the plane. Pop Pop said to Pierre instead of the plank to find two flat bits of wood about two feet long and getting some wide bandage out of his box, he gently straightened Stan's leg, a very painful operation! When Pierre came back with a flat piece of wood, part of an orange crate, Pop Pop put one piece at each side of Stan's leg and gently bandaged it to give him some support.

The next job was to get Stan into the harness so they could lift him out of the cockpit. This they did with much lifting and heaving and finally he was ready to move. Tying the rope on and pulling it through a hole above him, he asked Pierre to pull at the same time as Pop Pop, and he gently lifted Stan up and through the door and down onto the sand.

Stan felt a lot better by now and was propped up against the float in the shade. Stan said to Pop Pop "Get up into the plane and hand me down the radio earphone and speaker and turn the black knob to emergency mode." He then started to call "May day, may day," until he finally heard someone answer. He told them what had happened and asked for a rescue sea plane and gave them a map reference.

Now it was getting so hot. Pop Pop and Pierre got back into the plane to get the basket with the drinks and food and they sat on the floats, first looking after Stan the pilot and then themselves. Stan said what a good job they had done getting him out of the cockpit, and what a good thing Pierre had said to bring Pop Pop's box of tricks.

Then Stan heard the radio calling again and picked up the earphone to listen. The operator at the other end said they would have to stick it out for a couple of days as the rescue plane had not returned from another trip.

Pop Pop said, "If you are comfortable, Pierre and I will go and look around the island," and taking a bottle of water with them they set off.

They stayed on the beach as it wasn't a very big island, so that it would only take them a couple of hours walking to get around and back to the plane.

In the middle was a patch of palms and scrub and quite a few birds flying and sitting in the trees. They also noticed lots of turtle tracks where at night they had travelled the beach to lay their eggs in the hot sand.

Pop Pop said "I wonder where the birds got their drinking water from?"

Pierre said, "I bet there maybe a water hole in the trees."

So they trudged over to the trees and there in the middle was a water hole, not very big, but enough for the birds to drink from. There were also lizard tracks, but he didn't see any.

After about two hours they arrived back at the plane and asked Stan if he was still comfortable he said "Yes." He asked if they had found anything and they said yes and told him about the water hole and the turtles and lizards, also that there was a lot of driftwood around the island.

Pop Pop said "We have to make sleeping arrangements as it gets very cold at night."

Stan said he would be better if he stayed outside as he didn't think he would be able to get back in the plane.

Pop Pop and Pierre gathered lots of driftwood to make a shelter and a fire which they lit as it was getting towards evening time by now. They also made a shelter for Stan as Pop Pop and Pierre would sleep in the plane on the seating. "I suppose we ought to look at the food supply to see what we could cook." Said Pop Pop. So they got out the basket, but there was nothing to cook only cold food.

Pop Pop said "Is there anything to make a fishing line with?" Pop Pop looked into his box of tricks and found some line and some bits of wire maybe to make a hook out of. The next thing was what to use for bait? Pop Pop looked in the basket and found some bits of meat in the sandwiches.

Pierre said "Do fish like ham?"

"let's try with what we have." Replied Pop Pop. He threw the line into the sea and before long they had landed a big fish. Pierre was jumping up and down with delight. Pop Pop gutted it and soon had it on a stick roasting over the fire.

It smelt so good and before long they all had a portion to eat with the rest of the food in the basket and a drink to wash it down. Pop Pop also found that there were coconuts and bananas growing on the island. He picked some bananas and asked Pierre to wriggle up the tall coconut trees and knock down several nuts which he did. They were quite heavy to carry as they still had the copra on, which had to be cut off to get at the nuts inside. Pop Pop and Pierre arrived back at the plane and Stan was asleep so Pop Pop said to Pierre "Don't wake him, as he has had a rough time with his leg."

Inside Pop Pop's box of tricks was a large knife that he used to chop off the copra, which was green shell and very hard. Pretty soon Pop Pop had chopped off the shell and had only to break open the nut so that they would have a drink and some nut flesh to eat. As they sat by the plane eating the nut, Pop Pop heard the radio crackling and reached to answer it.

The rescue operator said to Pop Pop that the rescue plane, another sea plane, was on it's way and would be with them in about two hours. By this time Stan had woken up and asked Pop Pop what was happening and Pop Pop told him what the operator had said. Stan said he was pleased as his leg was hurting again.

After, Pop Pop gathered all the things that they had to take with them. Their cases and bags, Pop Pop's box of tricks, and Stan's things. They sat listening to hear if the plane was near and at last they heard the drone of an aircraft. Then they saw it circling around the island.

It finally landed on the sea and taxied up to within yards of the beach and two men, one a doctor, got out of the plane. The sea plane was much bigger than the one that Pop Pop and Pierre had travelled in, as they now had five people to travel and Stan had to travel on a stretcher. Coming over to them, the doctor examined Stan first and then Pierre and Pop Pop last. The doctor took off the makeshift splints that Pop Pop had put on Stan and was surprised at what a good job they had made of setting Stan's leg.

The pilot stowed all their baggage in the cabin and they lifted Stan, after the doctor had re-bandaged Stan's leg, onto the stretcher, and they all boarded. The pilot had to make out a report and looked at the damaged plane so they would return one day to dismantle it.

Taxiing across the water, they were soon in the air and flying back to base. They arrived much later and were told that as they had crash landed and were late for the lectures, they had cancelled the rest of the tour to Perth.

They were also told they had been booked into a hotel to rest before their flight back to England and Stan went off to hospital. The next morning at breakfast, the Australian newspaper men were waiting in the hotel reception to get their story and pictures, which appeared the next day.

Pierre said "I suppose we ought to keep a scrap book of all our newspaper reports and photo's."

Pop Pop said "What a good idea Pierre."

Back Home

After an uneventful journey home, a change for Pop Pop and Pierre, they arrived by taxi from the airport and walked around the side of the cottage to the back garden. Pop Pop couldn't wait to look as he had been away for so long. It was spring in Australia and autumn in England. A big smile crept across Pop Pop's face as he saw what a good job David had made of looking after his garden and must thank him later. He had brought back a couple of presents for his children in the cuddly toy like a koala bear and a kangaroo.

Pierre rushed into his tree house and opened the windows, as it had been closed up for several months. He had bought himself a scrap book at the airport and was keen to cut and paste all the newspaper photo's and cuttings he had collected and brought back with him. So Pop Pop went down to David's to give his children their presents and to thank him for such a good job he had made of Pop Pop's garden.

When he arrived back Pierre was still in his tree house, glue all over him and bits of paper all over the tree house floor. "What about some lunch?" said Pop Pop and went into the kitchen.

They had done some shopping on the way back. Pop Pop thought he would do beans on toast and called to Pierre did he want the same, he called out yes and Pop Pop said he had better come in and wash all the glue off his hands, other wise the knife and fork would stick to him.

After lunch the phone went, just as Pop Pop was dozing off in his rocking chair. It was the vicar of the local church, he asked if Pop Pop and Pierre would like to join them at the village hall as they were putting on a pantomime for Christmas and he wanted Pierre and Pop Pop to be in it with several other villagers.

Pop Pop said to Pierre "What do you think of the idea?"

Pierre said "it might be fun."

So they both said "Yes."

The vicar said "be down at the hall at 10am in the morning." "O.k.," replied Pop Pop.

When they arrived in the morning, the vicar said "Good morning" to them both. There were about thirty people there and they all said hello. The vicar said "All grab a chair and we will start our meeting." This they all did and he stood on the stage. "First of all," he said, "what pantomime would we like to do?"

One or two said what about Cinderella? Others said Puss in Boots and others said Aladdin.

The vicar said "Lets have a show of hands." So up went the hands to Cinderella 8 in all. Then 10 for Aladdin and 6 for Puss in Boots. "It looks as though Aladdin then." Smirked the vicar. "Now there are lots of different sets of clothing from other years and bits of scenery in the dressing room. Looks like we will have to go and sort through it all." He added.

Pierre said to Pop Pop "We will probably be the ones to make all the scenery, as we are good at building work and painting."

Aladdin was a pantomime that required a Lot of back cloth or scenery.

Pop Pop and Pierre had quite a few friends in business so it would be a case of can we have this or borrow that. Most times it was said with pleasure you are very welcome to it or you are doing me a favour to clear away someone's junk. So this was the way Pop Pop and Pierre got most of the scenery.

It took about a month to get what they needed to make the scenery. Also they had to find a magic carpet and a gene's lamp to make Aladdin's cave. The rest of the company were busy sewing altering old clothing and furniture. It was gradually coming together. At about midday, the vicar called everyone together to ask how it was coming.

Pop Pop said "Yes, but there are a few things still required. Like the music for the pantomime and a trap door in the floor so in case they had to make someone disappear."

They were talking about this when one of the helpers said "There is a trapdoor. It's under the carpet on the stage because they used it last year. If you go down under the stage you will see it."

The vicar said "It's so good of you all to give your time and work so hard. You do know it's for the children fund for all the children and families that need help in the village and children that are in hospital."

All the people said they were pleased to help as most of them were retired, so it gave them something to do and think about.

Pop Pop said to the vicar "I hope you will do some advertising in the newspaper, and you can use Pop Pop and Pierre's names to the publisher if you want, quoting who we are and what we had done in the past for children and our rescues."

The vicar thanked them and said he would.

The next day Pop Pop and Pierre were ready to erect the back cloth to the cave scene and get ready to paint. After that they had another six scenes to erect and paint. Each scene was painted on a curtain that would be pulled back as the tabs or stage curtains closed off each scene.

At the end of the day Pierre got paint all over himself, as he would work next to Pop Pop and Pop Pop's splashes dropped on to Pierre. So Pop Pop said "You go and work up the other end of the curtain and I will paint here."

At the end of November it was all coming together and the vicar was so pleased. Next they had to work out who was going to take each part and do some rehearsing. The vicar said a couple of days should see all the scenery finished, and then we can work out the parts and try on the clothing that had been made and altered.

How were they to work out the magic genie coming out of the lamp and a cloud of smoke?

Pop Pop came up with an idea. He said "If we make a big old lamp, big enough for Pierre to get into when Aladdin rubs the magic lamp, Pierre could appear and then Pop Pop would have a light shining on Pierre to cast a big shadow onto the curtain, with a puff of smoke. So it was decided that Pierre would be the genie of the lamp.

The vicar made Pop Pop the compare to open the show and to tell a few jokes.

What should Pop Pop wear?

They all said that he should wear a turban and turned up shoes and a silk robe and beard.

The next week was put aside for rehearsals and final preparations. On the Wednesday all the newspaper men turned up to do the 'write up' and to take pictures. Pop Pop said "It's going to be better than the west end play with the publicity they were getting in all the big newspapers!"

The vicar said "You'd better phone your son to get the tickets printed."

The church hall held 300 people Pop Pop said I hope it's a sell out so we will raise quite a sum of money for the children fund.

The other thing was the magic carpet. Pierre had worked it out with wires across the stage to make it fly across, with Aladdin appearing to be sitting on it. Aladdin of course also had a harness and rope from the top of the stage on runners.

The next day was Thursday, the day put back for dress rehearsals and then a rest day.

The Dress rehearsals went very well. Pop Pop came out to go through his jokes and patter, and the rest of the cast did their best. The vicar sitting out front said it all looked very professional. So everything was set for Saturday the big day before Christmas.

They had sold all the tickets, so it was a sell out which pleased the vicar and the press who were still around and some had bought tickets to the show. There was great excitement as Saturday came nearer and nearer. The vicar had been very busy within the local pub to provide a beer tent, with refreshments laid on for the half way interval.

So the great day arrived Pop Pop and Pierre woke up at six 'o' clock and went down to the village hall for final bits and pieces and a good look around and to oil the curtains and pulleys and to try everything out for the evening performance. They also tried out the music.

The show was to start at seven 'o' clock and lots of people had arrived early all dressed up and had gone into the beer tent where one of the players was selling programs. The vicar had the music playing and it was a lovely evening.

So at six forty five people started to drift into their seats to listen to the music. The vicar had also laid on girls with trays selling nuts, popcorn and chocolate bars, as there were quite a few children there. Seven 'o' clock arrived and everyone was dressed and ready. Pop

Pop looked at himself in the mirror and was satisfied with what he saw.

Pop Pop stepped out onto the stage with a big ovation from the audience. He started by saying, in his best speaking voice, "Good evening and welcome and thanks for buying tickets to the show for the children's fund." He then told a joke or two which went down well with much laughter.

The curtains went back and as they opened there was a bang and a puff of smoke and Pierre came out of the magic lamp. "No, no, no" Pop Pop shouted to Pierre "Not yet, your part comes later!" and also Pop Pop had a squeaky shoe as he walked across the stage, a roar went up from the audience they thought it was meant to be that way and part of the show.

The rest of the cast all played their parts and it went very well up to the interval. "Phew" Pop Pop said, "it's a good job the rest of the show went all right."

They stayed backstage and had a break and pretty soon the interval was up and back on stage for Pop Pop to open the second half, a few more jokes and the second half also went well with the magic carpet and the scenery looked so good.

It ended with all the cast being called onto the stage for a final bow. The audience gave them all a standing ovation, three in all. Most of the people stayed in the beer tent and some came back stage for champagne and to congratulate Pop Pop and the cast for the show.

The next day the critics write up and in the show column of the newspaper was very complimentary. 'Pierre and Pop Pop, a puff of smoke opens their show, as fifteen hundred pounds is raised for children's fund.' The pictures In the newspaper were of all the cast and Pop Pop and Pierre all dressed in their clothes for Aladdin. More cutting out for Pierre's scrap book.

Questions	Answers
How many rabbits are there?	
Who got rescued in the bus?	
Who wears a beret and is French?	
What was the name of the bird?	
Who did not like crabs?	
Who had a black face?	
What was the ghost?	
What did Pierre suck at the scout camp?	
Who fell down the well?	

The Garden Club

Spring was coming and the sun was getting warmer. Pop Pop and Pierre both love their garden as it makes a lovely relaxing place when they are not busy.

David, the father of young Billy they had saved from the well, belongs to a garden club in the village.

They meet once a week to read and talk about gardens, both vegetables and flowers and all sorts of other things.

Both Pop Pop and Pierre joined, as things in the school and the rescue side were a bit quiet after the adventures in New Zealand and Australia. They were glad of a break from travelling around the world.

The last meeting they had was a talk on harvest festivals, where they all had to grow and exhibit flowers and vegetables in the village hall and get prizes for the best and biggest at the show. Last year David won the best sweet pea flowers.

Pierre said to Pop Pop "What are we going to grow this year?"

Pop Pop said "What about the biggest marrow" Pierre said "Is there a prize for the smallest person growing the smallest carrot or something?"

Pop Pop said "I don't think so but we will find out at the club later!"

The quest was on.

They had lots to think about, Pierre said he was going to get lots of flowers around his tree house, things that climb up the trees. Cold and windy days they spent looking at seed and plant books with a pencil and paper planning what they would do. They also decided to harvest some of the fruit, vegetables and eggs that they didn't use.

Pierre said "We could have a stall at the market if we had enough to sell."

Pop Pop said "That's a good idea!"

Pierre said "I could grow French onions all tied together like we do in France." He decided to write to his uncle in France who had a small holding near Paris, to ask him to send over some special seeds, and any tips that he knew.

The front garden was all lawn and they didn't spend a lot of time out at the front, It's a good job as whenever they had work to do at the front Pierre would spend more time talking to people passing by, so Pop Pop ended up doing most of the work.

The back garden was very big with many fruit trees, including apple, pear, cherry and plum. They also had a large vegetable patch and lots of chickens. Pop Pop said to Pierre that he wouldn't have any time to spend in his hammock this year as there was a lot of work to do in the garden before the harvest festival.

After spending time sorting out what seeds to buy and what plants to plant, Pierre had his list for the garden centre. The next morning they set off for the garden centre with their lists, when they arrived they were amazed at the huge amount of trees and plants displayed all around the centre. Pierre went off on his own to look at the climbing plants for his tree house also at the banana, monkey puzzled trees and the seed counter.

Pop Pop said before he left "We will meet up at the cafe for some lunch and a drink at lunch time, roughly one 'o' clock!" Pop Pop had decided he would go in for mostly flowers and some vegetables, something like growing a giant marrow.

When they finally met up at the cafe later, Pierre said he had bought his seeds and also some sun flower plants. They had lunch and decided they would return home to do some planting in the afternoon. They spent all afternoon preparing the soil for the seed beds and had to make up lots of strings with bits of shiny tin-foil to keep the birds away.

Pierre planted his sun flowers by his tree house and also a climbing plant called a clematis, which when it flowered would cover his tree house with lovely pink, red and white flowers.

Pop Pop made his marrow bed under the cherry tree with lots of leaf mould and fertiliser to make giant marrow's and also planted his flower seeds. It was quite dark by the time they had finished. They both went in to make some dinner. Pierre was so excited he said he would get up early to see if his seeds had come up. Pop Pop said "They take quite a time to germinate, maybe a week" Pierre had no patience to wait!

Within three weeks most of the seeds were up and looking good.

Pop Pop said to Pierre "Don't let the chickens out otherwise they will scratch the seed beds up looking for worms, you're cousins I suppose."

Pierre said "I won't otherwise they may mistake me for a garden worm!"

David came up to look at what they were planning and said "Well done." He brought Pierre some special fertiliser for his sun flower plants. He said "It will make them grow ten feet tall."

Pierre said he could play Jack and the beanstalk on them. The next meeting of the garden club they had to decide and list what flowers and vegetables they would grow and exhibit. This was so the exhibition didn't end up with all the same flowers and vegetables otherwise the show would not be very interesting if everyone grew marrow's and sweet peas.

Whilst they were at the garden club they looked into the show cabinet at all the cups and shields and rosettes presented for the best and the biggest.

Pierre said "I am going to win one of those!"

Pop Pop said "I hope you do." Pop Pop said to himself he would never hear the last of it if he did. He would probably want a show cabinet in his tree house and Pop Pop would have to make it, more work!

The weeks and month's went by with lots of work in the garden. Everything was up and growing fast. Pop Pop's marrows were getting bigger and bigger until one day Pierre rushed in to say to Pop Pop "Come and look at you're marrow it is so big you won't believe it."

Pop Pop rushed to his marrow patch and saw the marrow as big as a football. Pop Pop couldn't understand it as he had only looked at it the day before. Pierre had blown a green balloon up and painted it with stripes and tied it to the plant, with that it went BANG!! Pop Pop chased Pierre up the garden laughing. Pop Pop thought what could he do to get his own back on Pierre.

That night he got some green string with some artificial sunflowers and put it all around Pierre's tree house so when he got up in the morning, he got his own back. Pierre didn't laugh as I think it was too early in the morning. He said "I am not a morning person Pop Pop." Pierre said he would leave the sunflowers where Pop Pop had put them until the real ones grew and flowered.

All the seeds and plants were growing and the flowers forming into buds. It was only two weeks to the show, now Pop Pop and Pierre had to sort out the flower buds and pull off the ones they didn't want, they only wanted the biggest ones for the show. It was the same with the marrow's and other vegetables So that all the growth went into the ones they had selected.

Pop Pop and Pierre walked down to David's house to look at his garden. His sweet peas and cosmos flowers were so colourful and it looked as if he might win again this year. David said to Pierre

"How are you're flowers growing?"

Pierre said that special compost was doing the trick and that he was very pleased so far.

So the day before the show arrived, and it was early to bed as they had to be up at day break to cut and display all the flowers and vegetables.

The alarm went off just as the sun was coming up and Pop Pop shot out of bed and called out to Pierre to get up quickly as they had a lot to do. Yawning Pierre came in from his tree house, got himself some breakfast and went out into the garden to start work. The first thing Pop Pop did was to lay out the trays for the vegetables and the tins with water in them to arrange the flowers. Pierre took his cutters to select his sun flower blooms and his carrots, he had to scrub and bunch them up for display.

Pop Pop cut his marrows and laid them in a tray with the parsnips and said to Pierre not to forget his strings of onions hanging on the kitchen door. He had made up the string the night before just like they do in France. Pierre said he would wear his beret at the show to look the part.

At the village hall there were tables laid out, each table had a name on it, so Pierre went off to find a card with their name on it. He soon found it and he called Pop Pop over to show him.

It was right near the entrance. Unknown to Pop Pop, Pierre had made a model of his tree house so that he could display his sun flowers up it just like at home and when he had finished it looked wonderful. So far, looking around the tables, Pop Pop's marrow was the biggest!

What a show! People gasped as they came into the entrance and saw Pierre's display with his onions and carrots all displayed in front of his tree house model and him with his beret on.

Pop Pop thought he better make just a good a show as Pierre. He made up a sign and also had books displayed that he was writing about their rescues and escapades and Pierre's scrap book.

The hall was pretty full by now and the judges were walking around looking and writing down the marks awarded. Pop Pop spent a lot of time signing books that he sold.

The judges finally arrived at Pop Pop and Pierre's table, Pop Pop got second prize for his marrow and first prize for his parsnips. Pierre got first prize for the best display of the whole show for the model tree house and sun flowers. Pierre also got a prize for wriggly carrots he had grown in special culture to give them a wriggly worm shape and he had stuck some buttons on for eyes. The judges had a good laugh and said to Pierre and Pop Pop "Well done!"

And who do you think won the best sweet pea prize?

Young Billy's dad, David.

In the evening's Pop Pop has to listen to Pierre's story about how he won the best display cup over and over again. Pierre has it sitting on the fire place shelf right in front of Pop Pop's arm chair.

The Snow Storm

Pop Pop had a phone call rather urgent one day to travel up to Scotland to look into his family tree on his mother's side, who were the Donaldson's and Scottish.

Pierre said he would like to come up with him so they both packed a bag. The weather forecast wasn't very good, snow was in the air. Pop Pop said "You had better bring some warm clothes with you and your hammock as it will be a long journey, also some food and drink"! Pierre made some soup and put it in a flask and packed a blanket.

They had spent a couple of days traveling and had stopped at a hotel to rest. On the evening of the second day the sky looked full of snow and very yellow. Just a few flakes at first and then big flakes blotting out the windscreen and the wipers.

Pop Pop said, we will have to stop as I can't see to drive any longer! They stayed in the car and had some soup and sandwiches, but it was still snowing very hard. Pop Pop used his mobile phone to ask the AA for the long range weather forcast, they said very bleak for at least three days. Pierre kept wiping the snow off the windows with the windscreen wipers. Pop Pop noticed where they were parked there was a big woods perhaps a forest.

As the wind was blowing very hard and in between the gusts Pop Pop saw what looked like a cottage in the woods. They had driven for miles and it was a very lonely spot. Pop Pop said we have been sitting here for four hours so they better make a move and look to see if the cottage was occupied. "Get your big coat and beret on Pierre and we'll go and have a look" getting out of the van was a job as the snow had built up deep snow drifts against the van. But pushing hard they managed it. Pop Pop put Pierre in his pocket and trudged over to the cottage.

The cottage looked very much like red riding hood's grandma's cottage. Walking with a lot of slipping and sliding they finally got to the front door. Wiping the snow away from the window and trying to look in they heard a child crying and called out to let them know that somebody was outside.

The child said her name was Jean and that her mum had gone shopping and hadn't come back, she had gone early in the morning saying she would be back in one hour and that was six hours ago. She said talking through the letter box that she was very worried and frightened and that she was six years old and that she had a phone call from her mother who was stuck at the shopping center and could not get back to the cottage because of the snow.

Pop Pop said to her give me the phone number and he would phone her mummy. Pop Pop phoned her mum and said please phone the police who would tell her who they were, this she did and phoned Pop Pop back and spoke to Jean to say let them help. Jean said she would let them in which she did. Pop Pop and Pierre were very glad to get inside out of the snow and wind.

The little girl called Jean said she was very hungry as she hadn't had anything since breakfast. We'll soon put that right, so taking off their coats they got to work. Jean said her little dog was hungry and also her dolly.

Lets look to see what we have in the cupboards and the fridge. Jean said she liked beans on toast, so that's what they all had. The dog a Yorkshire terrier had a tin and some biscuits and the dolly had some dolly mixture sweets. Pierre said we better phone Jeans mummy to let her know that all was well and they got Jean to talk on the phone to say that she was OK and that she like Pierre as he made her laugh. Pop Pop put Jean and her dog to bed and Pop Pop got some blankets and settled down on the settee by the fire side, Pierre slept in the arm chair with his beret on in case of an emergency he said.

In the morning Pop Pop woke up to find Pierre, Jean and the dog and her dolly all cuddled up on the arm chair with Peirre, she must have crept down in the middle of the night, I expect she was missing her mummy thought Pop Pop. He said to Pierre well we can't travel on as the snow was still coming down hard and they now had a little friend to look after. Pop Pop phoned the police station to say all was well and that they would stay and look after little Jean until her mum returned safely.

Well it snowed and snowed and snowed pretty soon the drifts were up to the windows and Pop Pop couldn't see his old van at all. It looks as we have lots of food in the cottage and wood and coal for the fire so we don't have to worry about anything.

Pierre said" We will have to play some games" so while Pop Pop went outside to clear a path to the van with a shovel Pierre played with Jean and the dog. Pop Pop shoveled and shoveled until he finally came across the van. He started the engine so that it wouldn't freeze up and also to get Pierre and Pop Pop's suit case which he took back to the cottage. It was still snowing, Pop Pop remembered a year in 1963 when it was just like this storm, it lasted for weeks. Early next morning Pop Pop woke up with a start, something sounded different. He was right the wind had stopped blowing and all was quiet not just quiet but hushly quiet and the winter sun was shining. He took the sleeping trio some tea and told them to listen, they said he couldn't hear anything, 'That's what I meant" Pop Pop said. It's the last of the egg wegies just enough for one egg and toast. As they sat around the table Pop Pop said "I think there is a farm on the other side of the forest, we will try to get there as we have run out of eggs and milk."

When they were all dressed up with warm clothes. Pop Pop opened the back door and with a shovel dug themselves out to the back yard, he could see that in the Forrest there was only a scattering of snow, as the trees had it all on their branches. "Right" said Pop Pop "Follow me" which they did he said "be very quiet as there will be lots of wild life in the Forrest looking for food" Jean whispered "Oh look theirs a robin red breast and it looks so hungry," Pop Pop had brought some crusts from the toast and gave some to Jean. Jean said "Look" the robin came right over and perched on her boot peeking at the crusts.

Pop Pop said "Don't forget" very quietly they tip toed on. The hush in the Forrest was like magic no wind, no noise of any sort, except the crunch, crunch, crunch of their boots in the snow.

"Look", said Pop Pop whispering at the tracks of a fox and also some big bird tracks following the path. Pop Pop had many times walked in the snow in woods and forests, and felt the same thrill. Pretty soon they came to a clearing and there were quite a few rabbits digging and eating at roots. Pop Pop waved them on putting his finger over his lips for quiet. Pop Pop stopped quite suddenly and pointed, standing so majestically was a stag deer with his great antlers and two doe deer. It wasn't long before the deer picked up their scent or smell of them all and took off knocking lots of snow off the tree branches.

Then they came to the farm yard where they found the farmer digging like mad trying to get to the cows in the cow pens for milking. He saw them all and said "Please would you help as the cows should have been milked two hours ago", but he explained it had taken him a long time to get half way across the yard. They all grabbed shovels and brooms and after lots of digging they reached the doors. By this time the cows were mooing and lots of them were full of milk. The farmer said could you all help so he told them what to do, there were sixteen cows to milk. Pierre and Jean got some feed into their trough, Pop Pop helped get the milking machine going with the farmer. It took them all three hours hard work when it was all done and the milk was in the churns the farmer said "You best come in the house." The farmer's wife was a rosy cheeked lady who thanked them for helping her Joe and welcome. She said "Wash your hands and sit at the table" which they did. The lunch was steak and kidney pie and syrup pudding and custard, what a feast. Pop Pop told Joe and his wife about Jean and her mummy and how they had been driving up to Scotland to trace the family tree and then got snowed in and couldn't drive any further.

Jean said to the farmer how Pierre had rescued her and Pop Pop said "I was there as well!" and Jean said "Sorry Pop Pop" The farmer's wife gave them some eggs and milk, no charge as we had helped her husband with the milking.

Jean said "Thank you" for her lovely lunch so did Pop Pop and Pierre and saying goodbye trudged back to the cottage. The police phoned Pop Pop and said they would have to stay another day as the snow was still bad. Pop Pop said "It's ok, we will look after Jean and the dog" whose name was butch "for as long as it takes."

The next day the snow cleared up and they had a phone call from Jean's mummy to say that she would be back at 2 'o' clock that day - if she could get through. She arrived at three 'o' clock, which made Jean very happy and also Butch the dog, she couldn't thank Pierre and Pop Pop enough and said any time Pop Pop and Pierre wanted a holiday they only had to phone and say. Pop Pop gave Jean a signed book of their adventure and went on their way. They had to cancel their journey to Scotland and said they would do it another day. Another special rescue by Pop Pop and Pierre. Jean sent a lovely picture to Pop Pop and Pierre drawn by her at school to say thank you for looking after her.

The Firework Display

It was now October and time for Pop Pop and Pierre to think about going to the schools to talk about safety at home and play and also to talk about firework night as it wouldn't be long before bonfire night was here.

The chief of the fire brigade had Invited Pop Pop and Pierre to visit the head depot and said that as they were involved with safety, he had made them honouree members. They had a special badge and Pierre was given a fireman's helmet and jacket also one to Pop Pop. They even called one their tenders after Pierre. Pierre loved to ride on the fire engine ringing the bell In fact he got told off by the fire chief for playing tunes on It and singing as they went to practice.

Early In November the children had started to build bonfires on the waste land and gathered all the burnable boxes and paper. Pop Pop and Pierre had lectured to several schools about not to play with fireworks in the streets or at home as they were very dangerous, and to keep them In a box with a lid.

In their talks they also reminded the children that it was best to have a grown up letting off the fireworks and only use sparklers, but even they could burn your fingers. Pop Pop and Pierre were put in charge of the village display organised by he gardening club. It has to be a grand affair as people in the village had given money to spend on food, drink and fireworks. There was quite a bit of planning to do so Pop Pop said he had better have several people Involved and form a committee.

David said that the old pub had a lock up storeroom to store the fireworks safely until the fifth of November. Pierre had bought himself some sparklers and jumping jacks and put them in David's store, as Pop Pop said not to store them in his tree house. He put his own special mark on them which read, 'Pierre's Collection Do Not Touch.'

The big day soon arrived. Pop Pop and Pierre and the committee had lots of work to do with tables and chairs and a tent for a bar and in case of rain. Pop Pop made a frame of timber for the firework display and tables for the rockets. The committee decided that the guy forks should be a day event as well and if it was fine weather to have a bit of a fete, with stalls and a roundabout for the children. Pierre said "That's a good idea," as he liked roundabouts and liked to sit in the middle.

Somebody came up with a suggestion to have Scottish and Irish dancers as there were quite a few Scottish and Irish families living In and around the village. That meant Pop Pop and Pierre had to build a stage for the dancing and bagpipe playing.

"More work"! Said Pop Pop.

"Never mind it was all to do with happy families and children" Pierre said, "and he also loved to see the happy smiling faces.

The fire chief said he would send several men to help, which he did. They even brought a mobile stage that they had at the fire depot. This saved Pop Pop and Pierre a lot of work. They also said they would bring the old fire engines and old hat's and old things they wore years ago. It was going to be a great success.

"The more the "merrier " said Pop Pop.

Pierre said he was going to make some toffee apples as Pop Pop had lots of apples in his loft and he only needed sugar to make the toffee.

Saturday was the big day! Pierre was all stuck up with apples and toffee and all over the kitchen, everything he touched was sticky.

Pop Pop said he hoped he didn't get stuck In the fire engine.

It looked as though it was going to be a great success as schools rang Pop Pop to ask if they could come and bring their fireworks.

Pop Pop said "All our welcome."

The committee had put the firemen in charge of the firework display for safety. Saturday dawned with the promise of a fine day cold, but dry.

Pop Pop said "I have never seen so many people gathered together in one place before"

Pierre said "All the better as they were charging a small entrance fee" Pierre had to sit at the entrance and collect the money and give a ticket, all the money was to go to the village children's fund and Red Cross.

The day started with dancing on the stage with bagpipes and a whistle band. What a sight they were and the press were there from the local newspaper taking lot's of pictures. Whilst this was going on the firemen let the children climb all over the fire engine. The whole of the field was busy with roundabouts and stalls selling bits and bobs and all sorts of fair ground stalls. Everybody was smiling and licking ice cream and toffee apples that Pierre had made. Pop Pop helped Pierre on the gate with tickets, whilst Pierre took the money and gave change.

The firework display was to start when it was getting dark which wasn't very late in the winter time, about five 'o'clock. After sitting at the gate all day Pierre said he was fed up of sitting and handed over to one of the committee ladies to collect the money.

Pop Pop and Pierre had been elected to light the fire, so with the fire brigade band playing 'Lets light up the sky' Pop Pop lit the torches. They were long sticks with tar on the end. They walked out and lit the paper and cardboard boxes and up it went cracking away and really lit up the sky.

What a day everyone was having and now the grandest of firework displays was starting. It was a dry night so there was a big crowd, lots of the crowd were singing to the band.

The fire chief and his men went out to start the display, first lighting the display on the timber frame which Pop Pop and Pierre had built, as the fireworks spread it spelt out the words "HAPPY GUY

FORKS DAY" and everybody cheered.

The big fire was burning brightly and creeping up to the guy on top of the fire with plenty of sparks blowing in the wind. With so many fireworks to light the firemen were so busy and what a show it was, as the rockets went up everyone shouted "Ooh, Aah".

They were about half way through the display when Pierre said to Pop Pop "It looks to me that their is another fire burning over there" and everyone was shouting, 'the old fire engine had caught fire!' One of the rockets had gone into the open window and set the firemen's clothing on fire. Now the firemen had a double job to do. Pop Pop ran over to ask all the people to stand well back as the engine had petrol in it's tanks.

The fire chief didn't know what to do as they had all driven to the grounds on the old fire engine. Now how to get back to the fire station to get another fire tender and water. Luckily the local policeman had his car parked near by so he took two of the firemen back to the fire station.

It took a good half hour before they returned and by that time the old fire engine was well alight. They arrived back just in time to save the petrol tanks going up, as that would have been very dangerous to all the people gathered around. It would have been like a bomb going off with a lot of people getting hurt.

The other firemen still carried on letting off the rest of the fireworks and everyone had a great time. It was midnight by the time all the fireworks had been let off and gradually people went home with smiling faces. All had had an enjoyable day except the firemen who had left their change of clothes in the old tender and also their wallets.

In the morning the show ground looked like a battle ground with the burnt out old fire engine all blackened.

The next day in the local paper, with pictures, was a write up of how Pierre had saved the day and diverted an explosion of the old fire engine. The paper had donated a fund for the firemen's loss of wallets and clothing, so they were smiling as well.

The Shamrock Holiday

Pop Pop had an invitation to go to Ireland to visit a friend in Dublin, who he had known from when he was in the army years ago. He said in his letter 'come for as long as you want as we have plenty of room.' When he left the army he had opened a horse riding and training stables outside Dublin.

Pierre asked if he could he come, as he liked horses and used to ride in France when he lived there. Pop Pop said he wouldn't go without him, as they were partners and friends for ever.

Pierre said "Will we see any little folk and banshees?"

Pop Pop said "I expect so." Pop Pop told Pierre all about when he was in the army and was billeted at barracks. He explained that his friends name was Philip and had a nick name of Banjo. Pop Pop never found out why, until somebody told him he played the banjo and was very good at it. In fact years ago he played in a band with three other people and had toured around the country.

The band was called 'the string quartet' and was very good.

Pierre said "Does he still play?"

Pop Pop said he didn't know and that he expected that he was too busy looking after his horses. "Horses take a lot of work and time." He said. Pop Pop went on to tell Pierre how he used to travel up to Stranraer in Scotland and then across to Larne in Northern Ireland on a ship. "It took a long time on the train in the war." He said.

Pierre said "Are we going on the same journey?"

Pop Pop told him no, as it took too long and that they would fly over as it was too long a journey by sea and train.

Pop Pop phoned Banjo, to ask what date to come over and Banjo said "Please yourself!". So Pop Pop asked Pierre when he would like to go. Pierre said when it is warm, in the spring. So they decided to go in May when all the flowers were out. Pop Pop then phoned the airport and booked the tickets to fly on a Saturday

They arrived in Shannon airport and Banjo was there to meet them. Pop Pop introduced Pierre to him and he said that any friend of Pop Pop was very welcome and a friend of his.

As they travelled along, Banjo pointed out all the places of interest and very soon they were driving in the country side. Banjo said,"Not far now. As soon as you see an entrance with a sign over it in the shape of a banjo - that's my place!"

As they drove under the sign they could see what a wonderful spread Banjo owned. There were stables and lots of green pasture.

"What a smashing place to live," said Pierre.

"Not bad is it," replied Banjo. He had never been a boastful man. Banjo unloaded Pop Pop and Pierre's luggage and took them into his house. The house was mostly square with a veranda all the way round the outside, so whichever way the sun was shining, you could move and sit in the sun or out of the wind all day long.

Pop Pop and Pierre were very pleased as they had a suite of rooms and Pierre didn't have to sleep in his hammock.

Banjo said he liked his nick name as it reminded him of the days when he played in his band. Banjo added that in the morning he would take Pop Pop and Pierre on a look around tour of his property in his four wheel drive.

Pop Pop and Pierre were awake very early, as the banging of buckets and doors woke them. It must be Banjo feeding and watering the horses, Pop Pop thought to himself.

Banjo had never married, so he had a lovely Irish lady who came in every day and cleaned and cooked and would chat away in her 'sing song' voice, to anyone that cared to stay and listen. Pierre loved all that and whilst she cooked the breakfast, she would tell him all about the Irish folk, the little people and the superstitions.

Pop Pop went outside to see Banjo. Banjo said he liked Pierre with his French accent and found him a very interesting fellow.

Pop Pop followed Banjo round from stable to stable. As they moved along, they talked of the days when they were in the army together.

Pop Pop said to Banjo "Do you remember when you and lots of others used to climb onto the roof to watch A.T.S sunbathing on the roof,"

"Yes" replied Banjo, smiling. "And what about the Robin Adare's castle we were billeted in County Antrim."

"The castle with the hand over the entrance," Pop Pop added, "You mean when we used to jump out of the windows on the fire escape harness and drop to the garden then race up the stairs to have another go. What times we had".

Banjo and Pop Pop had forgotten all about breakfast until Bryony called out from the kitchen window to call them in. By the time they had washed their boots and hands and sat down, Pierre had had two portions of everything and said that he could stay there forever talking to Bryony.

After breakfast Banjo took them on a tour of the house, which was very big, and out to a yard to drive around Banjo's property.

It was vast. Pierre and Pop Pop were very lucky as the sun was shining and the country side so green.

Pop Pop said to Pierre "Good job you said come in May as all of April it rained and only stopped raining on the Saturday they arrived."

Most of Banjo's horses had been put out to grass and were so pleased to be out in the fields and sunshine and were kicking up their heels and racing around in short bursts. Banjo said he had had a good winter and no sickness at the stables.

Banjo took them all around the spread and then down to the river where all the horses come down to drink. When they stopped and looked down from the hill, Pierre said "Look at all the foals splashing in the shallow water of the river."

Pop Pop said he wished he had brought his camera.

As they drove along-side the rivers edge, fish could be seen jumping out at the fly's hovering over the water and at the same time, Pop Pop and Pierre said "I wish I had brought my fishing rod."

They all ended up laughing at Pop Pop and so did he. Banjo said that any time they would like to use the four wheel drive; he would use his smaller land rover. He said he had a map and tour guide in the house and would get it out when they got back to the house that evening.

After dinner Banjo put on some of his records and they all sat around drinking and listening. Pierre went out to the kitchen to talk to Bryony and helped her wash up.

The next day Bryony packed them a picnic lunch and they went off in the four wheel drive with the map and tour guide. Pop Pop said "Let's motor up to Waterford and go to the glass works," as he was interested in watching the men glass blowing.

They spent all day being taken around the works and show rooms and had their picnic in the gardens.

On the way back in the afternoon, after driving through several villages, they saw a sign that said 'Second right to model village'. Pierre said "Let's go Pop Pop."

When they got there, they were amazed at the number of people that were their walking around. The whole village was built at quarter size. The church, the cottages, the post office everything even the pub.

The Bees

Pop Pop and Pierre's garden was a picture of flowers this year. Pierre had become so interested in gardening it was a job to get him in for meals. His tree house was a picture, with climbing flowers. He had spent the winter painting his tree house and it looked so smart with hanging baskets. He had built a new ladder and had a table and chairs on the grass to have his meals on.

Pop Pop and Pierre spent all their time when it was warm, in the garden. Pop Pop's friend David, from what was a public house down the road, came up to have some lunch. Pierre had made a salad with lettuce, cucumber, radishes and celery from the garden.

Pop Pop had cooked a large ham and a chicken. Pop Pop said to David "Why don't you phone your wife to bring the children up for lunch." They all arrived and one came over to Pop Pop to tell him about a swarm of bees he had seen in the woods. Pop Pop had another friend who he used to work with who was a bee keeper and knew all about bee keeping. Pop Pop phoned him to tell him about the swarm in the woods. Frank said he would come around and bring his smoke gun. Pierre had made himself a net hat and face mask so he could go with Frank to the woods to watch what he was going to do with the bees. Pop Pop said he would stay a distance away and watch.

Frank put on his bee mask and walked over to the trees where the bees were swarming, taking his smoke gun and basket to put the bee's in.

First he lit the gun, which started to make smoke. "This," he said, "will make them sleepy."

Pierre was standing next to him watching, as he pumped the smoke over the bees. One or two bees were flying around Pierre and Frank and slowly a few more came to buzz around them.

All of a sudden a great band of them separated from the rest and started to fly off in Pop Pop's direction. Pierre shouted to Pop Pop "Look out the bees are coming, run for your life," which Pop Pop did. The only trouble was Pop Pop was trying to get to his van and get inside. So there was Pop Pop running like stink, with this great black swarm of bees catching up fast on him. Pierre and Frank were laughing at the sight of Pop Pop swinging his arms about and running towards his van. He just about reached his van at the same time as the bees and trying to get the keys out of his pocket, in he dived with several bees with him and closed the door puffing like mad.

About six bees were in the van with him, he was lucky as he had some hair spray in the van with him. He sprayed the bees with hair spray and this stiffened their wings so all they could do was glide. The rest of the swarm settled on Pop Pop's van, so there was Pop Pop stuck in his van with bees all over the windows and his bonnet. Frank and Pierre put the rest of the bees in the basket to take home to Frank's bee hive to make honey. Frank came over to Pop Pop's van and said stay there and after he had taken his swarm of bees home he would come back and rescue Pop Pop.

Pop Pop was getting a bit worried, as he had been in his van a long time and the bees were still all over his van. In a swarm of bees there is a queen bee and wherever the queen bee goes all the rest follow. Pop Pop could see the queen bee on his windscreen. First he tried tapping on the window but she wouldn't move, then he turned on the radio to see if that would move her. No! Then he tried shining his torch at her, no nothing would move her.

Pop Pop thought it's a good job he had his box of tricks with him, so he turned around to the back seat and opened his box of tricks. Now he thought what will make the queen bee move and take the rest of the bees with her. He looked in his box of tricks and he soon saw a rocket firework. He thought this should do the trick. Now, he thought, how am I going to use it, do I light it and throw it out of the window? I have to be careful as I could set light to the van, then we would have flames inside the van and bees outside. He put the rocket in the seat beside him and looked again into his box of tricks.

He had a rope and harness, a signal gun, a mobile phone, a first aid box, some string, some soap, a sewing kit, a box of matches and a packet of fruit gums. Pop Pop thought he would have one of them while he was thinking about what to do. By the time he had thought what to do, he had eaten the whole packet. Now he thought I could give them a fruit gum, no I can't I've just eaten them all. Well then I couldn't!

Then Pop Pop thought of a good idea, he could phone up the king bee and ask him to tell the queen bee to come home, no that's no good, thought Pop Pop, she hasn't got a mobile phone. Well what am I going to do, as Frank and Pierre haven't come back to rescue me, I must get rid of the bees. Pop Pop said to himself. I could go to sleep, or I could smoke a cigar, or I could get out of the van and make a run for it, No then the bees might follow me and I'll have them all over me. No better stay in the van. In the end he fell asleep.

He dozed for a while, then woke up with a start as one of the bees gliding around the van landed on his nose. He brushed it off with his hand and went back to thinking what to do next. He was getting very worried, as by the time he got home, David and his family would have eaten all the picnic chicken and ham.

The thought of the picnic made him very hungry, but as he had eaten all the fruit gums, he had nothing else to eat! He could have a match and cook one of the bees, no that's no good I've only got six bees in the van. It's a good job he had a bottle of water in the van as he was getting very thirsty and fed up.

Now, he thought, if I lie on the floor the bees wont see me and they may go home. So he laid on the floor and just at the same time Frank and Pierre returned to the van and looked in the windows to see if Pop Pop was alright. But when they looked in, there was no Pop Pop in the van.

Pierre said to Frank "I think the bees have eaten Pop Pop." "Oh dear!" said Frank.

"Best thing we can do is go back to the picnic and have a good feed and come back later on."

Pop Pop had dozed off lying on the floor and just woken up as Pierre and Frank were walking away from the van. He jumped up to blow the van horn and shout "I'm in here, I'm here".

Pop Pop was lucky as Frank and Pierre had just got to the edge of the woods, so when they heard the Van horn they came back. While Pop Pop had been asleep all the bees had gone home, flown off with the queen bee.

Frank and Pierre got into the van with Pop Pop and drove home.

"I hope there's some food left as I am very hungry." said Pop Pop.

As they arrived Pierre opened the van door and raced in to get himself some food. By the time Pop Pop got out of the van with his stiff legs and walked into the picnic, it was all gone. "No food left!" he said "You rotten lot. You have eaten all the food and left me none!"

Then they all started to laugh and as they pulled a table cloth off and there was some left for Frank, Pierre and Pop Pop.

David, and his wife and children, wanted to know what had happened to them, so, in between mouthfuls of chicken leg, Pierre told them all about the bee swarm, how the bees had chased Pop Pop to his car and how they laughed at Pop Pop.

Pop Pop said he wasn't ever going to eat any more honey!

THE END

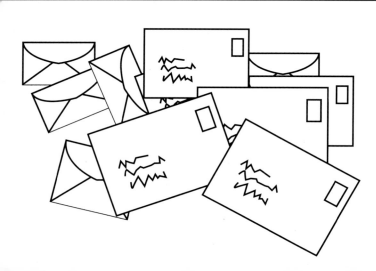